Contents

CHARACTER RECALL: THE SURVIVORS OF BLOOD SPURTS 2

Chapter One: The Morning After 5

Chapter Two: The Rules Were Never Real 9

Chapter Three: We Were Never Meant to Survive This 12

Chapter 4: The man in the room 15

Chapter 5: The hollow 19

Chapter 6: The eyes that stayed open .. 22

Chapter 7: The things we Bury 25

Chapter 8: Cracks in the Wall 28

Chapter 9: The Curator 31

Chapter 10: The Trap 34

Chapter 11: The Council's Truth 38

Chapter 12: The Breakout 42

Chapter 13: Gideon's Move 46

Chapter 14: Breaking Through 49

Chapter 15: The Pursuit 53

Chapter 16 – Fracture Point 56

Chapter 17 — The Break 60

Chapter 18 — Beneath the Surface 63

Chapter 20 — Crossroads at Midnight..69

Chapter 21 — The Breaker's Edge 73

Chapter 22 — Ghosts in the Ash..........77

Chapter 23 — Countdown.....................80

Chapter 24 — Firestorm.......................85

Chapter 25 — Detonation.....................88

Chapter 26 — The Final Confrontation .92

Chapter 27 — Burn It All Down 96

Epilogue 99

CHARACTER RECALL: THE SURVIVORS OF BLOOD SPURTS

Mike Halston

Then: A former Royal Marine turned student under a special veterans' program. He was the protector, the enforcer, the one who kept the group "safe" during their underground game nights. In Book 1, he became the unofficial leader when the fantasy crossed into murder.

Now: Hardened by guilt. Obsessed with truth. But still haunted by what he didn't see coming. Mike's greatest fear: he enjoyed the control too much.

"In the Corps, we hunted ghosts. But this? This was a ghost that hunted back." — Mike, Book 1

Mary Elson

Then: The university receptionist — not a student but drawn into the group via Debbie. Mary was older, quieter, the group's anchor — and the one who cleaned up the aftermath when things got messy. Her calm masked her secrets.

Now: Mary has doubts. About her past, her role, and her own memories. She thought she was just playing the game. Now, she wonders if she was always part of something much worse.

"I only kept the keys. I never asked what they opened." — Mary, Book 1

Debbie Lang

Then: The vibrant, reckless ringleader of the games. She created Blood Spurts — an underground dare system mixing truth-or-dare with pain, secrets, and escalating risks. She died in the hotel bathroom, throat slit — the first casualty of something darker.

Now: A ghost. A trigger. A symbol. Everyone sees her differently: martyr, manipulator, or first sacrifice.

"You play the game, or the game plays you." — Debbie, last known message

Sarah Lin

Then: The quiet one. An honours student, always watching. She never spoke much during the games, but she never missed a detail. When Debbie died, Sarah disappeared for days. When she returned, she knew things she shouldn't have.

Now: Sarah is the closest to the truth. She's the only one left un-compromised — for now. Her inbox is full of surveillance drops, whisper files, and encrypted warnings. The Archive has taken an interest in her — and she's not sure why.

"They didn't record me by accident. I was always part of the test." — Sarah, Book 2

Amy Velasquez

Then: The empath. The caretaker. Amy kept the group together emotionally — until she saw Debbie's body. She was the first to scream. The first to break. And maybe the first to be turned.

Now: Vanished. Either dead… or part of something else entirely.

"Pain was never the point. What we confessed under pain — that's what they wanted." — Amy, Book 2

Jane & Others

Then: Part of the peripheral players. Students, bystanders, dare-takers who never realized how far things had gone. In Book 1, some ran. Some were silenced. Others were "recruited."

Now: A few remain. Watching. Waiting. Or already compromised.

Chapter One: The Morning After

The dim morning light crept through the paper-thin curtains of the Briarwood Inn suite, brushing against empty bottles, ashtrays, and smeared glasses like a silent judge. The air was a slow, heavy fog of blood, sweat, and stale perfume. The floor was littered with cards from last night's game, red string bracelets, and half-scribbled dares that now seemed absurd in the quiet aftermath.

Bodies lay draped across furniture and tangled sheets—silent, still breathing, but far from peace.

No one noticed the time.

No one noticed the absence.

Until the scream.

It cleaved the silence like shattered glass.

Amy's voice tore through the room, brittle with hysteria. "Oh my God! No… NO!"

Mike bolted upright, instincts flaring. For a moment, disorientation dulled his reaction—until he saw her. Amy, framed in the bathroom doorway, shaking, her hands fluttering like broken wings over her mouth.

Mary stirred next, wrapping a sheet around her body. "Amy? What's wrong?" she croaked, already moving.

"I can't…" Amy choked, stumbling back. "It's… it's Debbie… she's dead."

The word rang out, stark and final.

Mike was on his feet instantly. He pushed past Amy gently but firmly. Her knees gave out, and she collapsed to the floor, sobbing.

The moment Mike stepped into the bathroom, he stopped cold.

Debbie lay in the tub.

Naked. Still. Blood soaked the porcelain, smeared in strange patterns, some dried like symbols, others still fresh enough to glisten.

Her wrists were slashed — deep, clean, like someone had done it with intention.

But that wasn't what made Mike stumble backward.

It was her throat — torn open, ragged and wide. Not a slice. A rending. Her head hung unnaturally sideways, nearly severed.

Mary appeared beside him. One look and her face drained of life. "No… no, we didn't… we didn't do this."

Behind them, the others gathered.

Jane gasped, turned, and vomited into a trash bin.

Mark stared blankly, lips moving without sound.

John slid to the floor, eyes glazed.

"What the fuck happened?" Mike growled, voice trembling under the surface. "She was fine last night. We were all fine."

Amy was hugging her knees now, eyes wide with trauma. "I woke up and she was gone. I thought she went to the bathroom… I didn't hear anything…"

"Did anyone?" Mary asked.

Silence.

The kind that thickens into guilt.

This wasn't the game anymore.

This wasn't a dare or a show of courage. This was real. Cold. Irrevocable.

Someone had crossed the line.

Mike turned to the group, eyes hard. "Nobody leaves. Do you understand me? Not until we figure out what happened. If we call the cops now—like this—they'll think it was all of us."

Jane looked up, her voice a broken whisper. "But she's dead, Mike. She's dead."

He nodded once. Grim. Steady.

"And if we don't get ahead of it, we all go down with her."

Outside, the first siren in the distance barely registered.

Inside, the game was over.

And the nightmare had begun.

Chapter Two: The Rules Were Never Real

Before the blood, there was a game.

They called it Blood Spurts. What started as a late-night dare between philosophy students and outsiders evolved into something much stranger. A social experiment. A cult of adrenaline. A closed loop of carefully managed chaos.

It was meant to test limits — physical, emotional, ethical. A mixture of truth-or-dare and ritual. Rule-bound. Secretive. Dangerous.

But not deadly.

Or so they believed.

It began during Mary's late shift as a university receptionist. She was older than most of the students, smart, careful, and a little too intrigued by the group's raw energy.

She watched from the sidelines at first. Then she joined. She brought structure. She enforced boundaries.

Mike entered next. Former Royal Marine. Quiet. Watchful. Drawn in by his younger cousin Debbie, who was always chasing extremes. Mike was supposed to be her tether. Instead, he became something else. The one who watched when others looked away. The one who saw things even he didn't want to understand.

Debbie was the nucleus. Bright, magnetic, reckless. She found a dusty folder in an abandoned psychology lab titled "Project Lamia." Inside: redacted studies, bizarre questionnaires, and notes on behaviour under duress. She turned it into a game. She made it theirs.

By Book Two, things had gone sideways. The group fractured. Surveillance footage emerged — of them, of others, of nights none of them remembered. A shadow figure named Gideon Rourke contacted Sarah, the quietest of the group, revealing that Blood Spurts had been monitored from the beginning.

It wasn't just a student game. It was a social contagion study. They were the data.

There were others. Watchers. Observers. Archivists. People with masks and cameras and silence. The group's rituals, pain-sharing challenges, even their supposed choices — all catalogued. Measured. Adjusted.

Debbie's death wasn't a fluke.

It was an escalation.

Book Two ended in the fog outside an abandoned observatory, where Gideon presented a metal box: The Archive. Footage, confessions, psychological profiles — even predictive models of their behaviour.

Mike, Sarah, Jane, and Mary chose to expose it. To break the cycle.

But when they left that night, Gideon whispered to his masked companion: "Activate the second archive."

Because this wasn't just about them anymore.

The experiment had grown.

Wider.

Darker.

Deeper.

And somewhere in the background, someone had rewritten the rules — not just of the game, but of what reality they were allowed to believe in.

Now, in Book Three, the fallout begins.

Chapter Three: We Were Never Meant to Survive This

The rain hadn't stopped in three days.

Sarah crouched beneath the collapsed eaves of the burned-out train depot, soaked to the bone and clutching the journal like it was still warm with blood. Somewhere behind her, a siren wailed — not police. Something higher, deeper. She'd heard it before.

It meant they'd found someone.

She just didn't know who yet.

Mary paced in the shadows, arms crossed tightly over her chest. Her coat hung from her like a funeral shroud. "They're closing in," she muttered. "We're not ghosts anymore."

Sarah said nothing. Her fingers had found a name in the journal again — Jane Elwell: Subject E4-03. Next to it, a note in tight, clinical handwriting: "Projected breach: 84%. Disposition: Redirect."

Mike emerged from the underpass, breath steaming in the air. "North access is clear. No movement. But they've got drones near the canal. Infrared. We're on a grid now."

"What about Jane?" Mary asked.

Mike looked down. "She's not answering."

Sarah felt the cold move deeper into her bones. Jane had always been the hinge. Brave enough to question, fragile enough to hide. If she'd gone dark, something was wrong. Worse than wrong.

"She wouldn't run," Sarah said.

"She might not have had a choice," Mike replied. Then softer: "Not all chains make noise."

They had tried to blow the lid off the Archive. Book Two ended with fire and fury — encrypted files sent to journalists, rogue data dumps across fringe servers, a desperate scream into a world that didn't want to listen.

But the story hadn't gone viral.

The Archive had absorbed the blow, silenced the leaks, swallowed the evidence.

And now, the experiment wasn't just continuing.

It was adapting.

There were new players in the game. Smiling professors. Hollow-eyed interns. Anonymous tipsters pretending to be whistleblowers. And always, always the Watchers — standing still just long enough to be seen, just long enough to haunt.

Mary sank down beside Sarah. "We need to disappear. Change names. Erase ourselves."

Sarah shook her head. "That's what they want. Witnesses who go quiet. Survivors who become myths."

"So what then?" Mary asked. "We keep playing?"

"No," Sarah whispered. She opened the journal, revealing the final page — blank, except for a single line written in red ink:

"The infection spreads when truth is suppressed."

Mike glanced at it and nodded. "Then we make it louder. Ugly. Unignorable."

He looked at them both. "We go to the press again. But this time, we don't stay anonymous."

Mary flinched. "You're saying we expose ourselves?"

Sarah's eyes were steel. "We already were. From the start."

A crack of thunder split the sky above them.

Somewhere, a camera lens blinked.

They stood together now — hunted, haunted, and fully awake.

Because this was no longer about secrets.

This was about survival.

And whoever had built Project Lamia was about to learn:

You don't control the fire once the match decides to burn.

Chapter 4: The man in the room

The rain struck the windows like fingernails tapping to be let in.

Sarah sat alone in her apartment, lights off, blinds closed. The only glow came from the cracked screen of her laptop, paused on an image she couldn't stop looking at: Gideon Rourke, captured mid-step outside the university's burned-out archives building. The timestamp read three days before Debbie died.

She'd seen him again last night — in person this time.

Not just some name buried in redacted documents. Not just a watermark at the corner of a surveillance feed. Gideon Rourke was real. And he had spoken her name like they'd met before.

But they hadn't... had they?

Two years ago —

The hotel suite had reeked of sweat, cologne, and expensive bourbon. Laughter spilled out of the room like static, wild and senseless. Sarah had stayed near the wall, always watching. Debbie had just finished her "Seven Blade Dare." Even the hardened ones — Mike, Jane, even Mary — looked shaken.

That's when the door opened.

No knock. Just a quiet, deliberate click. And in walked a stranger in a tailored charcoal coat, far too composed to be drunk, far too still to belong there.

Debbie's smile faltered. "Uh… you lost?"

The man said nothing at first. Just looked at them. One by one. Measuring.

Then he said it: "You've gone further than expected."

Sarah remembered the shift in the room — the sudden silence. As if something sacred had been broken.

Mike stepped forward. "Who the fuck are you?"

The man smiled. "You'll know me when it matters."

He turned to Debbie. "It's almost time."

Then he left, just as calmly.

They laughed it off later, mostly. Said it was probably a dare Debbie had set up, one more twisted layer to the night.

But Sarah never forgot his face. That precision. That knowledge.

Now —

She stared at his image. Older, but barely. Same suit. Same quiet authority.

Gideon Rourke.

He was no longer a mystery. He was a name attached to Project Lamia, to the ARGUS surveillance initiative, to the strange Blood Archive they'd uncovered beneath the university.

She reached for her phone and dialled Mary.

"Did you ever see him before that night?" Sarah asked.

Mary was quiet. Then: "Yes. Once. At the registrar's office. He was talking to the Dean, but… they never said his name. Just called him a 'consultant.'"

"From what?"

"I didn't ask." A pause. "Maybe I should have."

Sarah closed her laptop. She already knew the answer. Gideon wasn't from any department. He wasn't a student. He was the observer. The handler. The instigator.

He was the reason none of this had ever really ended.

And now… he was back.

Waiting.

Chapter 5: The hollow

Mike hadn't slept in two nights.

He'd tried. God, he'd tried. But every time his eyes closed, he saw it again — the tub, the blood, Debbie's lifeless grin. Her throat torn open like a confession scrawled in flesh.

And beneath it all: the rhythm of that first night. The game.

"Blood Spurts" had been a dare once. A twisted thrill between kids too clever and too bored for their own good. A secret society of scars and control. He'd told himself it was about limits — about owning pain instead of running from it.

But now?

Now it felt like a gateway drug to something older, sicker, and never meant for them.

He stood alone in his flat, shirtless, staring at the scar above his left collarbone — the one Debbie had carved herself. It used to feel like a badge. A memory of something electric. But now it just burned. A brand from a life he couldn't justify anymore.

He'd once been proud of what he called "tactical deviance." The ex-Royal Marine in him had believed pain was a pathway. That trauma, when chosen, forged bonds deeper than brotherhood.

But that night had broken something. Not just in the group. In him.

He could still hear the things Gideon Rourke had said in that fog-covered clearing. The man had spoken with the calm of someone who'd seen too much — or worse, engineered it. You were the match before I ever touched the fuse.

Mike didn't want to believe it. But part of him… knew it was true.

Because deep down, he'd liked it. All of it.

The blood. The hierarchy. The power.

And what did that make him?

Flashback — 18 Months Ago

The hotel suite was buzzing. The lights were low, and the dare wheel spun with a dizzying clack. Mary poured tequila shots with one hand while blindfolding Jane with the other. Debbie laughed — high and sharp — from where she stood atop the table, blade pressed to her thigh. The first cut always drew applause.

Mike sat on the edge of the couch, already drunk, already gone. But it was the adrenaline he'd been chasing — the crackle just beneath the skin when pleasure and danger brushed against one another.

That was the night he kissed Debbie. Right after she finished her third blood rite.

She'd tasted like metal and secrets.

"You're worse than me," she'd whispered.

And maybe she was right.

Now

Mike splashed cold water on his face, gripping the sink like it might run away.

"Focus," he muttered.

The group was unravelling. Sarah had gone dark. Mary was no longer playing defence. And Gideon? He was baiting them into something much bigger than they understood.

But Mike still had training. He still had muscle memory. He could protect them. If there was anything left to protect.

He looked up at the mirror. His reflection looked older, hollower.

He didn't recognize the man staring back.

Still, he whispered the same line he'd used on the battlefield — years before Blood Spurts had ever existed:

"Don't flinch. Don't look away. And never let the shadows move first."

It was time to call Sarah.

And it was time to finish this.

Chapter 6: The eyes that stayed open.

Sarah's POV

They were called the Watchers, but the name didn't do them justice.

To watch implied passivity — observation from a distance. But what the Watchers did… was curate.

Sarah stood beneath the flickering light of the underground archive vault, Gideon's box now cracked open in front of her. The metallic scent of old data — reels, tapes, USBs sealed in wax — filled the air with sterile rot. She flipped through the red journal again, its margins packed with notes in languages she didn't recognize, dates that stretched back decades, maybe longer.

This was where the rot had started.

This was where they had kept score.

Flashback // Excerpt from the Red Journal

London, 1972

"Initial tests successful. Psychological erosion occurs most rapidly between 18–26 years. Youth still believes in consequence, but has no immunity to myth. The introduction of 'The Game' catalysed spontaneous hierarchies, cruelty disguised as intimacy. We recorded everything."

"Phase One complete. Six candidates destabilized. Three retained."

The Watchers hadn't emerged in the first Blood Spurts. Not in the way Sarah now understood. Back then, their presence was background noise — a flicker of static in a forgotten corner of a recording, a streetlight that stayed on too long. Shadows that didn't quite match the figures who cast them.

But by the time Debbie died, the signs were there. Jane had mentioned strange emails that vanished after being read. Mike once caught a glimpse of a man in a charcoal coat watching from the rooftop. And Sarah… Sarah had found the first mirror glitch in the hotel hallway.

Only in Crimson Veil did the curtain begin to lift.

Gideon Rourke had given them names, but no identities. Only masks. Only rules. The Watchers didn't intervene. They provoked. They tested. They refined.

And worst of all: they kept everything.

Every twisted decision. Every whispered secret. Every drop of blood spilled in the name of thrill, ego, or desire. Archived. Categorized. Reviewed.

She turned to the adjacent wall where photos were pinned like insect specimens: blurry images of students, of them, caught in half-lit moments, unaware they were being studied.

What made it worse — what twisted the knife — was how subtle the manipulation had been. The game hadn't started because someone told them to. The Watchers had just made sure they wanted to.

Present Day

Sarah pulled the journal to her chest and stepped back into the cold hallway. The lights buzzed like hornets above her. Her breath clouded in the air. Somewhere above, a vent clicked open.

"They were never watching," she whispered to herself. "They were waiting."

And now?

They'd stopped waiting.

Chapter 7: The things we Bury

Mary's POV

She hadn't wanted to come back.

Not to the city. Not to the memories. And certainly not to the hotel.

But here she was again — five years later, standing at the edge of the same parking lot beneath a cloud-thick sky, staring up at the building where everything had gone wrong.

The windows on the fifth floor were dark now. Empty. Forgotten. But in her mind, that suite was still full of music, laughter, bad wine, and the giddy cruelty of young people who believed they were untouchable.

They called it a game.

Blood Spurts — part dare, part seduction, part ritual. It had started in whispers around campus. A challenge for those willing to play on the knife's edge of pain and pleasure. But by the time it reached Mike and Jane, by the time it reached *her*, it had already evolved into something more dangerous.

Something curated.

She knew that now.

But back then? Mary had just been the receptionist in the admin office, older than the rest, invisible to most of them. Until one day, she overheard Debbie talking about it — the "sessions," the "rules," the way people started to feel *changed* after playing.

And then she'd gotten the envelope.

No name. No return address. Just a folded card that read:
You've been selected. Curate or be consumed.

Inside was a list. Not of participants. Of *roles*.

Debbie — "the Catalyst."
Mike — "the Guardian."
Jane — "the Fracture."
Sarah — "the Observer."
Mary — "the Gate."

She didn't understand what it meant. Not until Gideon called her, not until he showed her the first file — footage of Debbie weeks before the game even began. Watching. Recording. Smiling into the wrong camera.

"She volunteered," Gideon had said. "But she didn't understand the weight. You can help guide the process. Minimize the damage."

Mary had agreed.

She told herself it was to protect them. She told herself she was a buffer, a failsafe. She told herself a lot of things.

But on the night Debbie died, Mary had stood in the hallway outside the suite for twenty-two minutes before entering. Listening. Waiting. Knowing *something* was wrong.

And doing nothing.

She hadn't known Debbie was already bleeding out in the tub. She hadn't known the Watchers were recording. But she knew the game had gone too far. And she knew Gideon would bury it, just as he always had.

Until now.

Now, Sarah had the journal. Now, Mike was asking questions. And the Watchers weren't hiding anymore.

Mary leaned against the wall of the hotel, heart hammering in her chest.

She had been the Gate.

But maybe it wasn't too late to shut it.

Chapter 8: Cracks in the Wall

Sarah's POV

Sarah found Mary on the rooftop.

She knew she'd be here — same place Mary always came when the weight of things grew too heavy. The cold wind tugged at Mary's coat as she leaned over the ledge, staring down at the shimmering city below.

"Do you ever think about jumping?" Sarah asked quietly, stepping up behind her.

Mary didn't flinch. "I used to. Not anymore."

Sarah folded her arms, watching the older woman. "You know why I'm here."

Mary let out a long, tired breath. "You want answers."

"I want the truth," Sarah said, her voice hardening. "No more circles. No more lies."

Mary straightened, finally turning to face her. "It wasn't all a game, Sarah. Not even in the beginning."

Sarah's jaw clenched. "You were there that night, Mary. You knew something was wrong before we did. Before Debbie…" She faltered, the word still sharp after all these years.

"I didn't kill her," Mary said softly.

"I never said you did."

Mary's lips curved into something bitter — halfway between a smile and a grimace. "But you wonder if I let it happen."

Silence hung between them.

Sarah looked down at the rooftop gravel beneath her boots. "We were just stupid kids."

"You were," Mary agreed quietly. "I wasn't."

There it was — the raw crack in the wall.

Sarah's fists clenched. "Why, Mary? Why did you get involved? You weren't like the rest of us."

"I was lonely," Mary admitted, voice thin. "I watched you all, every day, from my little desk in the admin office. You were alive,

Sarah. Messy, wild, reckless… and alive. I was thirty-five and invisible."

Sarah's throat tightened unexpectedly.

Mary's eyes glistened in the dim rooftop light. "So when Gideon came to me — when the Watchers offered me a place at the table — I said yes. I told myself I'd be protecting you. Guiding the group."

"But you didn't," Sarah whispered.

Mary shook her head. "No. I just watched."

The word sat heavy between them.

Sarah stepped closer, her voice lowering. "The journal says there was another phase after Debbie. That the experiment didn't stop with us. Do you know what they're planning, Mary?"

Mary's shoulders stiffened. "They're not just watching anymore, Sarah. They're preparing. You need to understand — Gideon was never the architect. He's just the curator."

Sarah's pulse quickened. "Curator of what?"

Mary's eyes darkened. "Human collapse."

Sarah's breath caught.

Mary placed a trembling hand on Sarah's arm. "We need Mike. We need Jane. And you need to decide right now — are you willing to burn it all down, even if it means burning us too?"

For a long moment, Sarah didn't answer. She stared past Mary, at the glowing skyline, at the faint wail of sirens below.

Finally, she whispered: "I don't think we have a choice anymore."

Chapter 9: The Curator

Gideon Rourke sat alone in the dim chamber beneath the old library.

The room smelled of cold stone and ancient paper, the walls lined with shelves holding dusty ledgers, reels of surveillance footage, and delicate red notebooks stamped with the Watchers' symbol — the closed eye.

He poured himself a small glass of whiskey, savouring the way the amber light caught in the cut crystal.

The Watchers had been here long before him. He was no founder — just another in a long chain of stewards. His job wasn't to command but to curate. To preserve. To document.

In Book One, Blood Spurts, the players thought they were acting on their own dark urges, chasing the thrill of pain, seduction, and risk. Gideon had been there in the shadows, nudging them along, recording the social breakdown, taking notes as each moral thread frayed.

When Debbie died, Gideon's original assignment was supposed to end. But something changed. The group hadn't shattered. They'd clung tighter. And when Sarah started digging, when Mike's military instincts kicked in, when Mary slipped behind the curtain, the Watchers saw an opportunity.

Book Two, Crimson Veil, escalated the game.

That phase tested not just individual collapse but ideological infection. Could Gideon introduce new fractures — through fear, through loyalty tests, through carefully planted lies? Could he push the group into destroying itself?

They had resisted.

Oh, they had broken plenty — but not in the ways the Watchers wanted.

So now came Book Three. The final phase.

He sipped his whiskey slowly, watching the monitor on the far wall.

Sarah and Mary on the rooftop.

Mike and Jane reassembling their fractured alliance.

The younger ones — Amy, Mark — drifting in and out of the edges, already half-lost.

Gideon knew the archive Sarah carried wasn't the archive. It was bait. It always had been.

The real treasure — the true experiment — was unfolding now. Could these humans, these fragile, clever, self-destructive creatures, choose truth over survival?

Could they expose everything, knowing it would destroy them?

His phone buzzed on the desk. A message.

Activate final protocol. Ready the second archive.

Gideon smiled faintly. The Watchers were ready to pull the curtain back entirely. Not just on this group — but on the whole system.

He stood, straightening his cuffs, feeling the weight of his carefully constructed mask settle over his face again.

For two books, he had been the man in the background, the cold observer. But in this final act, Gideon knew his own role was shifting. He was no longer just a curator.

He was the final test.

And when the last page turned, when the last betrayal fell like a hammer, Gideon Rourke intended to walk out of the ashes — not as the Watchers' servant, but as their master.

Chapter 10: The Trap

Mike crouched low behind the rusted-out car, his breath sharp in his ears.

The warehouse loomed ahead, its windows broken, its concrete walls slick with rain. The message had been clear:

Midnight. Come alone. Bring the journal.

But Sarah hadn't trusted it. Neither had Mike.

Now they were here, together, waiting in the dark.

"I don't like this," Sarah whispered beside him. Her fingers trembled slightly on the journal she clutched to her chest — the same blood-red book that had driven them this far.

Mike scanned the rooftop. No obvious sentries. But the tension in his gut told him they were walking straight into something.

"This isn't Gideon's style," Mike murmured. "He'd want to face us himself."

Sarah shook her head. "Unless he wants us to think that."

Lightning flashed distantly, briefly illuminating the cracked asphalt, the long-dead power lines sagging above.

Mike remembered the beginning — the allure of Blood Spurts, the high that came from stepping over moral lines, the feeling that they were untouchable. Back then, he'd been a thrill-seeker, a soldier still hungry for the edge.

Now? He felt hunted. Not by Gideon. Not even by the Watchers.

By something worse.

Sarah tensed. "Movement."

Mike followed her gaze. A figure had emerged from the side door — tall, hooded, face hidden. Not Gideon.

Another figure appeared behind the first. Then another.

Within seconds, five shapes stood at the warehouse entrance, forming a silent wall.

Sarah's breath caught. "That's not just Gideon."

Mike swore under his breath. "It's the inner circle."

The ones they'd only heard whispers about — the real architects, the ones even Gideon answered to.

Suddenly, the ground under Mike's boots felt very thin.

Sarah gripped his arm. "What do we do?"

Mike exhaled slowly. "We walk in."

Sarah's eyes widened. "Mike —"

He met her gaze. "If we run, they'll hunt us. If we stay, they'll crush us. But if we walk in — we might get one shot to break this."

Her jaw clenched. Then she nodded.

Together, they rose from cover, stepping into the open. The rain soaked through Mike's shirt in seconds, the cold biting down to his bones.

The five figures didn't move. They just watched.

When Mike and Sarah reached the door, one of the figures finally spoke — a woman's voice, low and cold.

"Mr. Bennett. Ms. Carter. You brought the journal."

Mike's hand hovered near his belt — no weapon, but the tension in his muscles felt like a drawn blade.

"Who are you?" Sarah demanded. "Where's Gideon?"

The woman's hood tilted slightly.

"Gideon was never the trap," she said softly. "You are."

Before Mike could react, the door behind them slammed shut.

The last thing he saw before the lights went out was the faint gleam of cameras —

dozens of them — hidden in the walls, the ceiling, the floor.

They hadn't been walking into a confrontation.

They'd been walking onto the stage.

Chapter 11: The Council's Truth

The room was silent except for the faint hiss of air through hidden vents.

Mike and Sarah stood at the centre of a wide, circular chamber — walls lined with black glass, the ceiling a dome of dull steel.

They could feel the eyes on them, though they saw no faces.

Suddenly, the room dimmed further, and a thin ring of light illuminated the platform where they stood.

A voice echoed, amplified, but unmistakably human.

"Michael Bennett. Sarah Carter. You've come far."

Sarah's fists tightened at her sides. "Where's Gideon?"

Another voice, softer, male. "Gideon has served his purpose. As have you."

Mike's jaw clenched. "What do you want?"

A panel on the far wall slid open, revealing a long table, and behind it, seven shadowed figures seated — the Council.

The inner architects of the Watchers.

One figure leaned forward slightly. "Do you know what this was ever about?"

Mike scowled. "Control."

Sarah spat, "Power."

The council figure gave a soft, almost amused laugh. "No. Understanding."

A second figure spoke, her voice sharp as glass. "For centuries, we've observed how humans unravel when tested. When presented with chaos, most collapse. But a few... reveal extraordinary patterns."

Sarah shook her head. "You murdered Debbie. You shattered lives."

The woman answered calmly. "We revealed what was already there. Blood Spurts, Crimson Veil — they weren't games. They were instruments. Trials to separate the noise from the signal."

Mike took a step forward. "And what signal are you looking for now?"

The first speaker stood, the light catching his pale, lined face.

"You, Mr. Bennett. You, Ms. Carter. You survived every phase. You adapted, you resisted, you fought. You were never just participants. You were candidates."

Mike froze. His heart pounded.

Sarah's voice shook. "Candidates… for what?"

The man smiled faintly. "For integration."

Behind them, the walls shifted, revealing massive screens flickering with data — faces, locations, live feeds of thousands, maybe millions.

"We are no longer content to observe from the shadows," the man continued. "The Watchers must evolve. We will shape, guide, and embed into the social bloodstream. And to do that, we need vessels. People the world believes are real. People with scars and stories — like you."

Mike's stomach turned. "You want us to be your front?"

Sarah's voice hardened. "Your puppets."

The council leader's eyes glinted. "Our avatars."

Suddenly, the floor under their feet vibrated. Mike instinctively reached for Sarah, pulling her close.

"We've mapped your networks, your habits, your drives," the woman said smoothly. "Everything you are has been recorded — replicated. Even now, we're already deploying the next phase."

Sarah's breath caught. "You don't need us."

The man smiled. "No. But imagine how much cleaner it looks if you stand on the stage and say you chose this."

The chamber doors sealed shut.

Lights pulsed on the far end of the room — dozens of Watchers stepping forward, masked, silent.

Mike squared his shoulders, heart hammering. "We're not giving you what you want."

The council leader's smile faded.

"No," he said softly. "But the world will."

The lights surged, and the Watchers closed in.

Chapter 12: The Breakout

Mike's pulse thundered in his ears as the masked Watchers closed in, their black-gloved hands reaching, their boots eerily soundless on the cold floor. He and Sarah were trapped.

They were under the old observatory, the original site where Blood Spurts' twisted experiments had begun years ago — but this was no abandoned ruin anymore. Beneath the crumbling dome, an entire hidden facility had been built, one they hadn't seen coming.

Sarah's breath hitched beside him. "There's no door," she hissed.

Mike scanned the walls — smooth black glass, no visible seams. The council sat calmly behind their glowing table, watching like scientists observing lab rats in a maze.

Mike's fists clenched. He wasn't going to die here.

"Sarah," he murmured, his voice low. "Remember the access tunnels they used in the early tests?"

She blinked at him. "The fire tunnels?"

"Yeah. There has to be one below this floor."

Sarah's eyes darted to the edges of the room — the faint lines where floor panels met. She'd been here before, years ago, as a test subject. She knew there were emergency passages, hidden out of sight.

But they'd have to get there.

Mike turned, meeting the gaze of the nearest Watcher. The masked figure was less than two meters away. Mike raised his voice.

"You know," he called to the council, "for people who claim to predict human behaviour, you've made one mistake."

The lead council member leaned forward slightly. "Oh?"

Mike grinned, teeth bared. "You forgot what happens when a cornered animal fights back."

Then he lunged.

His shoulder slammed into the Watcher's chest, knocking the figure back into another. Chaos erupted — the room flashing red as alarms blared, the Watchers trying to regroup, shouting commands into hidden earpieces.

Sarah dropped low, darting between two guards. She grabbed one of the metal rods from a belt holster and slammed it across the back of a knee. The Watcher fell with a sharp grunt.

Mike yanked another down by the mask, ripping it clean off — the young man beneath barely older than twenty, eyes wide with shock.

"Where's the floor access?!" Mike barked.

The kid shook his head furiously, terrified. But Sarah was already moving — she had spotted it.

"There!" she yelled, pointing to a maintenance hatch half-hidden beneath the council table.

Together, they ran.

Behind them, the council members rose in a slow, coordinated motion, watching with cold detachment as their prey scrambled for escape.

Mike grabbed the edge of the hatch and heaved — the metal groaned, the panel shuddering, but finally popped open. A narrow shaft yawned below, lit by faint emergency lights.

He shoved Sarah forward. "Go!"

She dropped in, sliding down the ladder as shouts echoed above.

Mike swung his legs over — but before he followed, he turned and locked eyes with the lead council member.

"We're not done," Mike growled.

The older man gave the faintest nod. "No," he murmured. "You're not."

Mike dropped.

The hatch slammed shut behind him.

Down in the maintenance shaft, Mike caught up with Sarah, their breath ragged in the tight space.

"Where does this lead?" he panted.

Sarah wiped sweat from her brow. "If the maps are right? Back to the surface tunnels. But we'll need to move fast — they'll be rerouting guards."

Above them, the faint sound of boots striking metal echoed down.

Mike took Sarah's hand. "Then we move. Now."

Together, they plunged into the dark.

They weren't just fighting to escape the council.

They were running to expose everything — before the Watchers could close the net for good.

Chapter 13: Gideon's Move

The night air was sharp atop the ridge overlooking the observatory. Gideon Rourke stood in the shadows, his long coat stirring in the wind, eyes fixed on the crumbling dome below.

His earpiece crackled softly.

"They've made contact," a voice murmured. "They're inside."

Gideon allowed himself the faintest smile. "Of course they are."

He checked his watch — a sleek black military model, synced to the countdown running in the background. The window was narrowing. If Mike and Sarah didn't break out within the next twenty minutes, the council's extraction teams would lock down the tunnels permanently.

He paced slowly, hands clasped behind his back.

For years, Gideon had played both sides. On paper, he was an independent operative — part consultant, part fixer, part saboteur. To the Watchers, he had been an external agent, brought in when things threatened to spill too far into public view.

But Gideon had never been fully loyal to the council. Not really.

He understood the original mission: monitor, test, push human boundaries. But over time, the council had turned into something else — an entity obsessed with control. No longer content to observe, they had started shaping events directly, curating chaos like curators arranging exhibits in a private gallery.

Gideon had seen enough.

He had picked his side months ago — and tonight, it was time to show his hand.

A soft footfall sounded behind him. He turned slightly as Ava emerged from the trees, her dark hair tied back, a pistol holstered under her jacket.

"They're in the south tunnels now," she reported quietly. "We can meet them at the secondary exit."

Gideon nodded. "Good. The council will block the main shafts first. We'll need to intercept before they flood the outer passageways."

Ava hesitated. "And the council itself?"

Gideon gave a thin smile. "They'll stay seated. They always do. They think they're untouchable in that room — but tonight, the data Mike and Sarah carry is the real threat."

His eyes flicked toward the glowing dome.

"Once they surface, we get them out of here," he said. "Then we leak everything. Names. Experiments. Locations. The whole archive. No more hidden hands."

Ava let out a slow breath. "You really think they'll let us live after this?"

Gideon's jaw tightened. "I don't care."

He checked his watch again. "Time to move."

Together, they slipped back into the forest, moving quickly down the ridge, following a narrow, overgrown path that led toward the old maintenance shafts.

Gideon's mind raced.

Mike had changed. Sarah had hardened. Even Mary — the old receptionist turned survivor — had learned to see past the lies. They were no longer just pawns in a twisted experiment.

But Gideon knew the council had one last card to play.

He could feel it in the air — that electric tension right before the storm.

As he and Ava reached the treeline, the first dull thud echoed from the tunnels below. Explosives. Forced blockades.

They were out of time.

Gideon clenched his fists.

"All right," he murmured, voice steeling. "Let's bring them home."

Chapter 14: Breaking Through

The air inside the tunnel was stifling, heavy with dust and the sharp scent of old stone and rusted metal. Mike's shoulders burned as he pushed a fallen beam aside, clearing the narrow crawlspace for Sarah to slip through.

She coughed, waving a hand in front of her face. "Mike, we don't have time to clear the whole passage. They're closing in behind us."

Mike turned, wiping sweat from his brow with a grimy sleeve. His chest heaved, muscles straining — but not just from the physical effort.

He could feel it: the old hunger, the pulse that once thrilled through him like fire in his veins.

In the early days — back in the first Blood Spurts — Mike had thrived on the edge. Former Royal Marine, adrenaline junkie, the guy who ran toward violence when others flinched away. The games, the blood, the sharp taste of control — it had fed something raw inside him.

But now?

Now he was tired.

Not physically — though the bruises and scars had accumulated — but in his soul.

He wasn't chasing the thrill anymore. He was running from the wreckage.

"Mike!" Sarah grabbed his arm, shaking him. "Snap out of it — I can hear them back there."

He blinked, shaking himself free of the spiral. "Yeah. Yeah, I'm good."

He wasn't good.

He was worn down.

They scrambled forward, squeezing through a side shaft, the old metal walls groaning as they brushed past. Somewhere deep in the tunnels, the Watchers' operatives were sealing exits, flooding passages. They had to be two steps ahead — or they'd end up trapped like rats in a maze.

Sarah glanced back at him. "You used to love this, you know."

Mike grunted. "What?"

"The danger. The edge. Back then, you'd have been smiling." She didn't say it cruelly — just an observation.

Mike let out a slow, shaky breath. "I know."

He paused, pressing his forehead briefly to the cool wall. "I used to think the blood was the point. That it made me sharp, made me alive."

He straightened, meeting her gaze.

"But now? I just want out. I want us out. No more deaths. No more games."

Sarah gave him a small, tired smile. "You're not the same guy anymore."

"No," Mike murmured. "I'm not."

A loud metallic thud echoed behind them — too close. Sarah jumped. Mike's eyes snapped wide, instincts kicking in.

"Move," he ordered, grabbing her hand. "Now."

They ran, ducking through the broken maintenance archway, lungs burning, footsteps echoing in the confined space.

The tunnel forked ahead — left or right. Mike hesitated for only a second before pulling Sarah right. He knew the layout better, remembered the old escape routes from long ago.

As they sprinted, his mind raced.

He wasn't hunting blood anymore. He was fighting for survival.

For Sarah. For the others.

For himself.

Ahead, a faint light glimmered — not the cold, sterile glow of the Watchers' equipment, but real light. Outside light.

"We're close," Sarah gasped.

Mike nodded; teeth clenched. "We just have to live long enough to reach it."

And as they surged forward, hand in hand, the echoes of his old self — the man who craved the crimson rush — faded behind him, step by painful step.

Chapter 15: The Pursuit

In the control van parked at the mouth of the tunnel system, a row of monitors flickered with grainy black-and-white feeds. Figures moved on the screens — two blips marked in red, deep inside the labyrinth.

"They're moving faster now," the lead Watcher murmured. His voice was smooth, almost detached. He tapped the glass gently. "Sector Four cleared yet?"

A younger agent at the console nodded. "Sealed five minutes ago. They're boxed in on three sides. Only one viable exit left."

The lead Watcher — codename PHANTOM — gave a small, satisfied smile. "Good. Herd them to the surface. Gideon wants eyes on them before they breach."

Behind them, another figure stepped into the van, rain dripping from the hood of her black jacket. Ava. Her eyes, sharp and calculating, swept the monitors.

"They're smarter than you gave them credit for," she murmured.

PHANTOM didn't flinch. "They're rats in a maze, Ms. Ava. They'll scramble, they'll run — but they'll still hit the traps."

Ava's mouth tightened. "Don't underestimate them."

Inside the tunnels, Watcher teams advanced methodically — helmets gleaming under headlamps, weapons lowered but ready. Their boots crunched over debris as they moved through the narrow shafts.

One team leader keyed his comm. "North approach secure. Negative on visual — target may have doubled back."

PHANTOM's voice crackled through the earpiece. "Negative. Keep pressure. Push them east."

In the shadows, a pair of agents paused at an intersection. Faint echoes rippled down the corridor — hurried footsteps, breathing, scuffing against the walls.

"Movement," one whispered.

The other raised his hand, signalling the team.

With surgical precision, they split into flanking positions. This wasn't the chaos of Book One, where brute force ruled — nor even the occult manipulations of Crimson Veil.

No, the Watchers had evolved.

They had refined their methods, honed their craft.

They were no longer observers.

They were predators.

Inside the van, Ava leaned closer to the monitors, watching Mike and Sarah's markers dart through the digital map. Her jaw clenched.

"They're heading for the south tunnels," she said quietly. "They know the old infrastructure better than you predicted."

PHANTOM tapped a screen, pulling up thermal overlays. "We predicted every variable. It's a controlled test."

Ava gave him a sharp look. "You're not the only one testing, Phantom."

The Watcher gave a faint smile but said nothing.

In the tunnels, the two figures kept running, unaware that the walls were closing around them.

Above ground, more Watcher units spread out, forming a loose cordon near the collapsed maintenance yard. Night vision scopes scanned the crumbling ruins, while drones hovered silently overhead.

The order was simple.

No escape.

Inside the van, a new voice crackled over comms — one that froze Ava mid-step.

"Council orders," the voice rasped. "Do not engage directly. Observe final interactions. Confirm subject parameters before retrieval."

PHANTOM's face darkened slightly. "Copy."

Ava exhaled slowly, her mind racing.

She had seen this before. Mike and Sarah weren't just running from death — they were running into something worse. Something the Watchers had been waiting to unleash.

Chapter 16 – Fracture Point

The cold air inside the maintenance tunnels stung Mike's lungs as he sprinted, Sarah close behind. Concrete walls flashed by under the flicker of their stolen flashlight, the echo of footsteps behind them no longer distant.

"They're closing in," Sarah hissed, clutching the satchel tighter against her chest — the satchel carrying the archive they'd risked everything to steal. "We can't outrun them forever."

Mike shot a glance back, his face pale but determined. "We don't need forever. Just five more minutes. Gideon said the hatch leads out by the river."

She almost laughed — not because it was funny, but because it was insane. Trusting Gideon Rourke had never been part of their plan. Not in the beginning, not even midway. And yet here they were, running on a breadcrumb trail laid out by the one man who knew more than he ever let on.

Above ground, Gideon watched the treeline from the edge of the abandoned parking lot, breath curling in the cold night air. His coat hung loose, one gloved hand holding a slim communication device.

"They're pushing too fast," he muttered into the mic. "Pull back the perimeter teams. Give them a path."

A voice crackled in his ear: "The Council won't like this."

"They never do," Gideon smirked. "But they hired me for a reason." He lowered the mic and glanced toward the blinking signal on his handheld tracker — two blips, moving fast, heading right toward the exit. Good. Let them reach it. Let them think they were ahead.

In the shadows across the lot, the Watchers waited. Masked figures, cloaked in heavy garments, their eyes reflecting the faint glow of infrared lenses. They were patient, calculating. The Council had grown them over two decades — evolving from mere observers into full enforcers, trained to monitor, extract, or erase as necessary. Where once they'd only watched, now they shaped outcomes.

Inside the tunnels, Mike's legs burned, his heart pounding in his ears. For the first time in months, maybe years, the old hunger — the thrill he'd once chased in the Blood Spurts days — was silent. No rush. No taste of violence on his tongue. Only fear. Only purpose.

He slammed his shoulder into the rusted hatch, the metal screeching as it gave way. Cold night air rushed in, and beyond it, the gurgling river stretched out under a moonless sky.

"We're out!" Sarah gasped, her eyes shining with raw hope.

Mike reached to pull her through when a figure stepped from the trees — Gideon.

"You're late," Gideon said, smiling faintly. "But you made it."

Mike's fists clenched. "You sold us out."

"No," Gideon said softly, holding up a hand. "I'm the only reason you're still breathing. Behind them, shadows moved — Watchers closing in, their steps soundless. On the ridge above, more figures emerged, and just beyond, a sleek black vehicle approached with two members of the Council seated inside, watching everything unfold.

Sarah's breath hitched. "What do we do now?"

Mike's voice was low, steady. "We end it."

The final confrontation had arrived — every choice, every betrayal, every buried secret now rising to the surface.

And the night had only just begun.

Chapter 17 — The Break

Mike's muscles tensed as the first Watcher moved into view, a sleek figure in dark combat gear, face hidden behind the silver mask.

"Hand it over," the figure said — voice modulated, almost inhuman.

Sarah gripped the satchel tighter. "Like hell."

Behind them, Gideon lifted a hand slowly, his eyes flicking between Mike and the Watchers. "Careful," he murmured, "if they wanted you dead, you'd already be on the ground."

Mike's heart pounded so hard he could barely hear. He knew that. He knew it. These weren't just enforcers — they were handlers. Trappers. The Watchers didn't move without purpose.

Sarah whispered, "Mike… what if he's part of this?" Her eyes darted to Gideon.

He shot her a look. "I know."

But they had no choice.

Suddenly, the sleek black vehicle pulled up closer, headlights snapping on. Mike shielded his eyes as the rear door opened — and for the first time, they saw her.

Amy.

Alive.

Her hair was shorter now, her face pale, sharper somehow — but unmistakably Amy. She stepped out, her thin hand raised calmly.

"Mike," she said softly, "Sarah. You weren't supposed to get this far."

Sarah's mouth dropped open. "Amy? You're... you're with them?"

Mike's stomach flipped. No.

Amy smiled faintly, stepping toward them. "There's always been more going on. Debbie's death, the Blood Spurts games, even Crimson Veil — all of it was curated. We were chosen."

Chosen. The word slammed into Mike like a punch.

"We were the experiment," Amy continued, voice steady. "But not all experiments fail. Some of us... graduated."

Sarah staggered back, shaking her head. "You're lying."

"I'm not," Amy said, her eyes glinting. "And the real twist? Gideon works for me."

Mike whipped around — Gideon gave a small, regretful shrug.

"I warned you to choose wisely," Gideon said softly. "You just kept chasing the wrong threat."

A ripple passed through the Watchers, a subtle shift as they raised their weapons — not to kill, but to seize.

Mike's blood roared in his ears. For a heartbeat, the old urge surged inside him — the hunger, the edge. But he forced it down. No. Not this time.

He grabbed Sarah's hand, squeezing hard. "We run."

Before she could respond, he pulled her sharply sideways — into the river.

Cold slammed into them, water dragging at their limbs, but they pushed through, fighting against the current.

Behind them, the Watchers hesitated — not wanting to risk the chase in unfamiliar terrain.

Amy's voice echoed faintly across the water. "Let them go. They'll come back. They always come back."

On the riverbank, Gideon watched them vanish into the dark. His jaw tightened.

Because in the end, the trap wasn't just physical.

It was psychological.

And the next phase had just begun.

Chapter 18 — Beneath the Surface

The cold bit into Mike's skin like knives. His lungs burned as he and Sarah broke through the river's surface, gasping for air. The night pressed heavy around them, the moon a pale smudge behind thick clouds.

Mike pulled Sarah toward the shore, both of them scrambling up the muddy bank, panting hard. His arms were scraped raw, but he barely felt it — the adrenaline drowned everything else.

Sarah collapsed onto her back, coughing water out of her lungs. "God… dammit, Mike…" she rasped. "You didn't even warn me."

He dropped beside her, chest heaving. "Didn't have time."

She shoved at his shoulder, weakly but angry. "You never give me time."

For a moment, they just lay there, staring up at the night sky, their bodies shaking. The river gurgled behind them, swallowing the noise of the Watchers regrouping on the far bank.

Mike turned his head toward her. "You okay?"

Sarah gave a shaky laugh. "Define okay."

Silence settled between them — but it wasn't comfortable. Not anymore.

Mike could feel the old fractures. Back when Blood Spurts started, Sarah had been a thrill-seeker, eager to push limits, always hungry for more. Mike had been drawn to that, pulled into the sharp energy between pain and pleasure, blood and control.

But now? Now, Sarah's eyes were different. Hardened. Not just thrill-seeking — battle-worn.

"You're mad," he muttered.

Sarah let out a humourless laugh. "Mad? I'm furious, Mike. We're up against an organization we don't understand, betrayed by people we trusted, running for our lives

— and you still act like you have to shoulder it all alone."

Mike bristled. "You think I wanted this? You think I planned for any of it?"

"No," Sarah snapped, pushing herself up, "but you always act like you have to be the hero. Like the rest of us can't carry weight."

Mike's fists clenched, then slowly relaxed. His shoulders sagged. "I'm just trying to keep you alive."

Sarah's face softened — just a flicker. "I know."

For a beat, the space between them pulsed with everything unspoken — the regrets, the buried anger, the history that tied them together tighter than they admitted.

Finally, Sarah said quietly, "We can't keep running. We have to outthink them."

Mike nodded. "Agreed."

They sat in the wet grass, shivering, listening to the distant hum of engines and shouts across the river.

Sarah drew in a slow, shaky breath. "You think Gideon let us go?"

Mike's jaw tightened. "No. He's counting on us coming back."

Sarah gave a bitter smile. "Then maybe it's time we stop playing the part they wrote for us."

Mike looked at her, something sparking in his eyes — the old soldier's fire, tempered now by something heavier: resolve.

"Then let's flip the game," he murmured.

In the distance, thunder rolled low.

And somewhere far away, the Watchers began setting their next pieces on the board.

Chapter 19 — Ghosts We Left Behind

Mike's fingers tapped out a rhythm on the cracked burner phone as Sarah paced the length of the damp motel room.

Outside, a neon sign buzzed faintly, casting sharp blue light through the dirty window. The room smelled of mildew and cigarettes, the kind of place where no one asked questions — perfect for fugitives.

"Are you sure about this?" Sarah asked, voice low, arms crossed tightly.

Mike didn't look up. "No."

She let out a frustrated breath. "You didn't answer back there when I asked if Gideon let us go. You don't think we escaped, do you?"

Mike finally raised his eyes. "He's still pulling strings. But if we're going to rip this out at the root, we need more than just the two of us."

Sarah sank onto the edge of the bed, hands clasped. "Who, Mike? Who's left?"

He clicked the last number, hesitating a heartbeat before hitting send. "Jane."

Sarah stiffened. "You trust Jane?"

"I trust she hates Gideon more than she hates me," Mike said grimly.

The line crackled, ringing once… twice…

"Mike?" The voice on the other end was sharp, familiar, layered with both exhaustion and suspicion.

"Jane, it's time."

A pause. Then a bitter laugh. "Didn't think you'd live long enough to say those words."

Sarah leaned forward, whispering, "Put her on speaker."

Mike clicked it over. "Sarah's here."

Another pause. "Well, well, the golden girl survives. Colour me shocked."

"Jane," Sarah cut in sharply, "this isn't a reunion call. We need help. We're going after Gideon, but the Watchers are closing in fast."

Jane's voice hardened. "You're just now figuring out they never stopped watching? The council's been moving assets for weeks. You two are just the last to realize the walls are closing."

Mike rubbed a hand over his face. "Then come in. Help us crack this open."

A long silence on the line.

Finally, Jane spoke quietly. "You're not the only ones left, you know. There are others. Ones who broke away, who've been waiting. But you'll have to convince them you're not leading the Watchers straight to their door."

Sarah exchanged a look with Mike. "We're past convincing. We're down to desperation."

Jane gave a short, grim laugh. "Good. Desperation is the right place to start."

She rattled off a meet location: an abandoned subway entrance two cities over. Midnight. No weapons visible. No surprises.

As the call ended, Sarah exhaled slowly. "Do you think they'll actually show?"

Mike stood, tucking the burner into his pocket. His face was hard, but his voice was steady.

"They'll show," he murmured. "Because if they don't, Gideon wins."

He crossed to the window, looking out into the cold night. For the first time in a long time, his chest felt lighter — not because the threat was gone, but because for the first time, they weren't alone.

Behind him, Sarah rose, pulling on her jacket.

Together, they stepped back into the storm.

Chapter 20 — Crossroads at Midnight

The abandoned subway entrance yawned open like a mouth swallowing the city. Broken tiles littered the cracked concrete steps, and rusted gates sagged on twisted hinges.

Mike scanned the shadows. Midnight sharp. No sound except the drip of water somewhere deep below.

Sarah shifted beside him, her eyes flicking nervously over the graffiti-scrawled walls. "I don't like this."

"Neither do I," Mike murmured.

A sudden flicker — movement near the tunnel mouth.

Jane emerged from the darkness, her silhouette sharp, coat flaring behind her like a blade. She wasn't alone. Two figures flanked her, faces hooded, silent, watching.

"You made it," Jane called softly. Her voice echoed.

Mike stepped forward, hands raised. "We came alone. Just like you said."

Jane gave a small, bitter smile. "For once, you follow instructions."

Sarah narrowed her eyes. "Where are the others?"

Jane shrugged. "Waiting. Watching." She gestured to the two hooded figures. "These two came as… insurance."

Mike's gut tightened. He didn't like this.

Jane tilted her head. "You know, it's funny. All this time, you thought Gideon was the master behind the curtain. But here's the truth, Mike — the real master has been sitting inside your little circle since the beginning."

Sarah froze. "What are you talking about?"

Jane smiled wider. "You still don't get it?"

One of the hooded figures stepped forward, pulling back their hood.

Amy.

Alive.

Sarah's breath caught. "But... you died. Debbie... you were..."

Amy's eyes glittered cold. "I survived. And I learned. Gideon? He's not the only one pulling strings. He was just phase two. I'm phase three."

Mike felt the bottom drop out of his stomach. "You were working with the Watchers."

Amy smiled softly. "Not working with. Leading."

Jane gave a small, mock-apologetic shrug. "Surprise."

Sarah's fists clenched. "Why?"

Amy stepped closer, her voice almost tender. "Because none of you ever understood. The game was never about survival. It was about evolution."

Suddenly, floodlights blazed on around the tunnel mouth. Dozens of masked figures — Watchers — emerged from the shadows, weapons raised, surrounding them.

Mike spun, heart hammering. Sarah grabbed his arm.

Amy's smile widened. "You were never running from the Watchers, Mike. You were running straight to me."

Jane's voice turned cold. "Welcome to the final phase."

For the first time, Mike felt something crack inside his chest. Not fear. Not rage.

Betrayal.

He locked eyes with Sarah.

And in that breathless second, they both knew — they were going to fight.

Even if it meant burning everything down.

Chapter 21 — The Breaker's Edge

Mike's fists curled, every muscle coiled tight. Sarah's hand tightened on his arm, her breath ragged.

All around them, masked Watchers closed in, weapons glinting in the harsh white floodlights. Jane stood to the side, calm and smiling like a snake. Amy stepped forward, head held high, eyes glowing with triumph.

"You really thought you'd outplay us?" Amy said softly. "All your scrambling, all your running — we've been ahead of you since the hotel. Since before Debbie."

Sarah's voice came out low and sharp. "Debbie died because of you."

Amy's smile faltered for half a second. "She was… necessary."

Mike felt his vision narrow, rage pounding like a war drum in his chest. He shot a glance at Sarah — a silent agreement passed between them.

No more running.

No more games.

Without warning, Mike lunged.

He slammed his shoulder into the nearest Watcher, knocking the man off balance. Sarah moved with him, sweeping low to grab the dropped weapon. She fired — the crack of the shot slicing through the stunned silence.

Chaos exploded.

The Watchers surged forward, weapons raised. Mike grabbed a baton from the ground, swinging hard, cracking it across a masked face. Blood sprayed. Sarah spun, dropping another guard with a clean shot to the leg.

Jane cursed and ducked back, pulling out a radio. Amy's face twisted in fury.

"Take them down!" Amy screamed.

Mike grabbed Sarah's wrist, yanking her toward the side tunnel. "Move! Now!"

They sprinted, boots slamming against the concrete, ducking under rusted beams and leaping over old debris. Behind them, gunfire erupted, bullets sparking against the walls.

They burst into an old maintenance room — metal lockers, shattered lights, dust thick in the air. Mike shoved the door shut, jamming a pipe through the handle.

His chest heaved. Sarah's eyes were wide, hair plastered to her face with sweat.

"They were never going to let us walk," Sarah gasped.

Mike slammed his fist against the wall, frustration roaring in his veins. "We're outnumbered. Outgunned."

But Sarah was shaking her head, her lips curving into a tight smile. "Not outsmarted."

She pulled something from her coat — the small black device Gideon had slipped to them back at the river.

Mike's eyes widened. "The detonator."

Sarah nodded grimly. "Gideon said… if we ever needed a real distraction."

Outside, they heard the shouts, the pounding of boots.

Mike looked at Sarah, something fierce sparking between them.

"Ready?"

Sarah's thumb hovered over the button.

"Let's burn their whole damn game down."

She pressed it.

A low rumble shook the walls.

Outside, muffled shouts turned to screams.

Mike grabbed Sarah's hand, pulling her through a back hatch as the floor buckled. Behind them, fire bloomed — a roar of light and heat tearing through the tunnels.

The old subway collapsed in on itself, the Watchers' command centre reduced to rubble.

As they emerged, breathless, into the night air, Mike turned to Sarah.

"This isn't over," he said, eyes fierce.

Sarah nodded, her smile grim. "No. But it's our turn now."

Somewhere far off, Amy watched the smoke rise, her eyes narrowing.

Phase three had failed.

But she wasn't done yet.

Not by a long shot.

Chapter 22 — Ghosts in the Ash

The night air bit cold against Mike's skin as he and Sarah moved quickly through the shadows, their breath clouding in the dark. The flames behind them were still crackling, the Watchers' stronghold buried beneath smoking rubble.

But Mike knew better than to believe it was over.

Sarah touched his arm gently, her face pale but determined. "They'll regroup. Amy… she's not the type to go down with the building."

Mike gave a tight nod. His pulse was still pounding, adrenaline searing through his veins. "She's always three steps ahead."

As they crossed a narrow bridge, an old warehouse loomed ahead — the place where Gideon had told them to meet if things went south.

But the windows were dark.

The door hung slightly open.

Mike motioned for Sarah to stay back, creeping forward with a practiced carefulness, his old Marine instincts humming to life. He pushed the door slowly, slipping inside.

The smell hit him first: smoke, metal, something faintly chemical.

Then he saw them.

Bodies.

Two Watchers — masks shattered; throats slit clean.

Gideon was gone.

On the far wall, a message was scrawled in blood-red paint:

"Too slow."

Mike's fists clenched. His jaw tightened.

Sarah slipped in behind him, eyes going wide at the scene. "No… Gideon…"

Mike touched the edge of one mask, flipping it over. The hollow black eyes stared back. He felt the weight settle heavier on his shoulders.

"We're not just running from Amy now," he said grimly. "She's started cutting away the pieces she doesn't need."

Sarah shivered. "She's cleaning house."

A sudden sharp noise made them both whirl — the soft crunch of a boot on gravel.

They spun around, weapons raised — only to see a figure step calmly from the shadows.

It was Gideon.

Alive.

Barely.

His face was pale, blood streaking down one side. He limped forward, clutching his side. "They knew," he rasped. "Amy knew I'd meet you here."

Sarah rushed to his side, helping steady him. "We thought you were dead."

Gideon gave a thin, grim smile. "Not yet."

Mike narrowed his eyes. "Why spare you? Why not finish it?"

Gideon's expression darkened. "Because she wanted to send a message. And because she's already setting up the final stage."

Mike's heart sank.

"The final stage?" Sarah asked, voice tight.

Gideon nodded slowly. "She's planning to broadcast everything — every tape, every archive, every dirty secret we ever thought we buried. Not just about the Watchers. About us."

Mike felt the weight of it hit his chest.

The hotel. Debbie. The games. The blood.

If Amy unleashed it, they were all finished.

"We stop her," Mike said quietly, his voice like steel. "Whatever it takes."

Gideon smiled faintly. "Then you'd better hurry."

Because somewhere, not far away, Amy stood before a bank of monitors, her finger hovering over the control panel, the countdown already ticking.

Chapter 23 — Countdown

Amy's reflection shimmered faintly in the polished glass of the control room, her pale face lit by the flicker of dozens of screens. Across every monitor, the same image pulsed — a spinning countdown clock, glowing red against black.

00:29:59.

She smiled, tapping one manicured finger against the console.

Outside the reinforced glass, the last of her loyal Watchers were fanning out, securing the perimeter. She could hear their muffled voices through the headset, calm and certain.

They had no idea she was about to leave them all behind.

Amy stepped closer to the terminal. She reached into her coat pocket, pulling out a small silver device — a modified pulse key. One touch, and every archive, every file, every corrupted secret from the last three years would flood onto the public net.

The governments wouldn't be able to bury it. The Watchers wouldn't be able to spin it.

And Mike?

He'd burn with the rest of them.

Her fingers hovered above the activation pad.

At the edge of the compound, Mike crouched behind a shipping container, sweat beading down his back despite the cold. Sarah pressed close behind him, her breath sharp in his ear.

"She's in the main control room," Gideon whispered over the comms. "But listen, Mike — this isn't just about stopping her. It's about what comes after. If you take her down, you'll be the face they turn to."

Mike gave a bitter smirk. "Yeah, well, I'm not sure I'm leadership material."

Sarah touched his arm. "We're with you. Always."

Mike closed his eyes briefly. That warmth — that anchor — it steadied him in a way no weapon ever could.

Then he snapped his eyes open. "Let's go."

Inside, Amy watched the final seconds bleed away.

00:02:11.

She inhaled slowly, savouring the moment.

"Do you know," she murmured, her voice soft as silk, "what it's like to control the story?"

The door behind her slammed open.

Mike.

Sarah.

Amy turned, her eyes glittering. "You're too late."

Mike lifted his weapon — but Amy only smiled, holding up the pulse key between two fingers.

"Shoot me," she said, "and this drops. The broadcast triggers automatically."

Mike's muscles coiled, his mind racing.

Sarah's voice was low, urgent. "Mike… think."

Amy's smile widened. "You never learned, did you? This was never about survival. It was about transformation."

00:00:30.

Mike took a slow step forward.

Amy's hand twitched, hovering over the final button.

"Did Debbie scream?" Mike asked softly.

Amy's eyes flashed. "She sang."

Sarah gasped.

And Mike moved.

Not forward — but sideways.

He slammed his elbow into the main console, driving it down with all his strength. Sparks exploded; the panel burst in a shower of light. Amy shrieked, jerking back — but the pulse key flew from her hand, skittering across the floor.

Sarah dove.

Caught it.

The timer froze —

00:00:03.

Amy's breath hitched.

Mike stepped closer, his face grim. "It ends here."

But Amy's smile came back — slow, feral.

"Oh, no, Mike," she whispered. "You just triggered the real game."

Above them, the ceiling split open — metal grating peeling back to reveal rows of black drones, eyes flickering red, humming to life.

Mike's stomach turned to ice.

Sarah's voice cracked. "Mike…"

And somewhere across the compound, Gideon's voice cut through the comms, sharp and panicked:

"RUN!"

Chapter 24 — Firestorm

The first drone shrieked as it dove, a spear of red light slicing through the smoke-filled control room. Mike yanked Sarah down just in time, the heat of the beam searing past his cheek.

The room erupted into chaos. Sparks rained from the shredded ceiling, cables snapping like whips, alarms blaring in a rising, hysterical chorus.

Amy was gone — she'd bolted the second the drones came online, slipping through a side exit before Mike could stop her.

"Get up!" Mike barked, hauling Sarah to her feet. She was clutching the pulse key so hard her knuckles were white.

They dashed through the control room's side door, skidding into the dark corridor beyond. The compound's walls shook as the drones swarmed, crashing through the air vents, tearing through the reinforced security layers like paper.

"Gideon!" Mike shouted into his comms. "Where are you?"

Static.

Then Gideon's strained voice: "Evac point — west platform — move, NOW!"

Mike grabbed Sarah's hand, pulling her into a sprint. The corridor pulsed red with emergency lights, shadows flickering in the corners.

Behind them, a drone smashed through the steel door, twisting and shrieking, eyes blazing.

Mike spun, firing — one, two, three sharp bursts — but the rounds barely dented the machine's armoured chassis.

"We need heavier firepower," he growled.

Sarah yanked him toward the far end of the hall. "Storage room. I saw it earlier — come on!"

Inside the storage room, they slammed the door shut and braced it with a steel bar. Sarah darted to a crate, yanking it open. Inside: a stash of old Watcher tech — EMP grenades, pulse disruptors, specialized rounds.

Mike grinned, teeth flashing. "Now we're talking."

He loaded a disruptor shell into his rifle, shoving an EMP grenade into Sarah's hand.

The door shook violently.

Mike raised his rifle, took a breath — and nodded.

Sarah yanked the door open, hurling the grenade down the hall. A blinding pulse of blue light lit the corridor, and the pursuing drones faltered, their systems sparking wildly.

Mike charged out, dropping two more drones with precise shots. Sarah followed, heart hammering, lungs burning.

On the west platform, Gideon was waiting, flanked by two battered Watcher defectors.

"You're late," Gideon said coolly, though his sharp eyes flicked nervously to the sky, where the drone swarm was circling.

Mike strode up, tossing the pulse key into Gideon's hands. "We've got maybe five minutes before this whole place goes up."

"Good," Gideon murmured, pocketing the key. "Let it burn."

Sarah stared at him. "What?"

Gideon smiled thinly. "The only way to break the Watchers is to destroy their roots. We end it tonight."

As if on cue, Amy's voice crackled over the platform loudspeakers — cool, triumphant:

"Leaving so soon? Oh, come now — I've got one more surprise."

The platform rumbled. Beneath their feet, the floor split open, revealing a vast, black chamber — and rising from its depths, a monstrous machine, bristling with weapons, its core pulsing like a heartbeat.

Mike's blood turned cold.

Sarah gasped.

And Gideon whispered, almost in awe, "She built a failsafe."

The machine's eyes flared red.

Amy's voice purred: "Let's play."

Chapter 25 — Detonation

The monstrous machine roared to life, gears grinding, limbs unfolding, weapon arrays locking into place. Its core pulsed once, twice — then unleashed a blinding arc of energy that tore across the platform, shearing steel like paper.

Mike tackled Sarah, shoving her behind a concrete pillar just as the blast ripped past.

"Gideon!" Mike bellowed.

But Gideon was already moving — sprinting across the open space, coat whipping behind him, a small device clutched in his hand. He darted between the machine's scanning beams, heading straight for its exposed flank.

Sarah scrambled up beside Mike, breathless. "He's insane — that thing will kill him!"

"No," Mike growled, eyes locked on Gideon. "He's betting everything on one shot."

Above, Amy watched from a glass control room, her face illuminated by glowing panels.

"Poor Gideon," she murmured, her fingers dancing over the console. "Still thinks he's the hero."

She leaned closer to the microphone.

"Mike… I know you're listening."

Mike stiffened, teeth clenched.

Amy's voice was soft, almost regretful.

"You were always the best player. I really did admire you. But you should've walked away when you had the chance. " Gideon reached the machine's flank, slamming the device onto its armoured plating. A green light blinked. One second. Two.

Suddenly, the machine twisted, slamming a massive mechanical arm down. Gideon rolled aside — barely — but the device was crushed under the blow.

Mike's heart stopped.

Gideon looked up, blood on his face.

Their eyes met across the platform.

And Gideon smiled.

He raised one hand — revealing a second detonator.

Click.

The ground shuddered. Deep below, a chain of buried charges erupted, shaking the entire facility. Explosions roared through the walls, tearing through foundations.

The monstrous machine reeled, systems faltering. Sparks shot from its joints, its red eyes flickering wildly.

Mike grabbed Sarah's hand. "We run. NOW."

Together they sprinted, dodging falling beams and shattering glass as the platform buckled.

Gideon, bleeding and staggering, limped after them.

Overhead, Amy slammed her fists onto the console, screaming.

"No! NO!"

Behind her, the control room's windows cracked, fire licking up the walls.

Mike, Sarah, and Gideon burst out into the open night just as the entire compound erupted in a towering fireball, the shockwave hurling them to the ground.

For a moment, there was only silence — the sky above glowing with smoke and burning debris.

Mike pushed himself up, coughing hard. Sarah lay beside him, dazed but alive.

Gideon knelt a few feet away, face streaked with ash, shoulders shaking.

Mike staggered over, gripping his arm. "Did we do it?"

Gideon looked up, eyes hollow.

"I don't know."

From the burning wreckage, a dark figure emerged — walking calmly through the flames.

Amy.

Alive.

And she was smiling.

Chapter 26 — The Final Confrontation

The heat from the burning compound washed over them, waves of blistering air that made Sarah's eyes sting and Mike's skin crackle with sweat.

Amy stood at the edge of the inferno, her silhouette sharp against the pulsing firelight. Her once-pristine blouse was torn, hair wild, but her eyes — those cold, calculating eyes — gleamed with triumph.

"You really thought you could outplay me?" she called, her voice smooth, almost amused. "After everything we've been through, Mike, you still don't understand."

Mike squared his shoulders, stepping forward. "I understand you killed them. All of them. You used us. You made us pawns."

Amy tilted her head. "You were pawns before I ever arrived. I just made you see the board."

Sarah hissed under her breath, fingers tightening on the small pistol she'd scavenged from the wreckage. "She's stalling."

Mike nodded once. "Yeah. But why?"

Gideon, limping up beside them, grimaced. "Because she's not finished yet."

Suddenly, the earth trembled — a low, rumbling vibration. From the ruined compound, a massive shape emerged, dragging itself free from the rubble.

The Watcher Prime.

A towering construct, larger than anything they'd faced before. Its body was a grotesque fusion of steel and bone, mechanical limbs bristling with weapons, its central core a pulsing, crimson eye.

Amy turned slightly, smiling at the monstrous machine. "Meet the next phase."

Mike's stomach twisted. "You've got to be kidding me."

Sarah raised her gun, but Gideon put a hand on her arm. "That's not going to scratch it."

Amy stepped forward, lifting a sleek control device. "You see, Mike, you were the test.

The rest of them? The students? Mary? Even Debbie? Just proof of concept. But you…" She smiled. "You made it real."

Mike clenched his fists.

Sarah whispered, "We need a plan."

Gideon's eyes flicked across the burning wreckage. "There's only one."

The Watcher Prime roared to life, weapons locking onto the three of them.

And Mike ran.

Straight at Amy.

Sarah shouted, "Mike, WAIT—!" but he was already moving, sprinting at full speed, every muscle straining.

Amy's eyes widened — just for a split second — before Mike slammed into her, sending both of them crashing to the ground.

The control device skittered from her hands, bouncing across the dirt.

Gideon dove, snatching it up. "I hope you're ready to gamble, Mike!"

The Watcher Prime charged, engines howling.

Gideon jammed the device into its frequency port.

Mike pinned Amy to the ground, their faces inches apart. "Checkmate."

Gideon hit the button.

A high-pitched shriek filled the air — a piercing electronic wail that split the night.

The Watcher Prime convulsed, limbs jerking wildly. Sparks exploded from its joints, its crimson eye flickering, fading…

…and then, with a final grinding howl, the machine collapsed, shaking the earth as it fell.

For a heartbeat, everything went still.

Amy's smile was gone.

Mike let out a long, shuddering breath, feeling the weight of everything they'd survived.

Gideon stood beside him, face pale, eyes haunted. "It's over."

Sarah joined them, slipping her hand into Mike's.

Amy lay in the dirt, defeated, her eyes burning with quiet fury.

But somewhere in the shadows, unseen, another figure watched — one none of them had noticed.

And it smiled.

Because some games never truly end.

Chapter 27 — Burn It All Down

The sky roared with fire.

Flames licked up into the black night, towers of orange and gold twisting into the clouds like the arms of some angry god. The compound — once a fortress, once a sanctuary, once the heart of the Watchers — was now a smoking ruin.

Mike ran, Sarah right behind him, heart hammering in his chest like a war drum. Every breath tasted like ash. Every heartbeat thudded like a countdown.

Gideon sprinted alongside them, clutching the data drive against his chest — the drive that contained every secret, every lie, every betrayal going back decades.

Behind them, the wreckage of the Watcher Prime collapsed in on itself, each metallic groan echoing like the death knell of an empire.

"We have to move!" Sarah shouted, coughing through the smoke. "It's going to blow!"

"Almost there!" Mike barked, eyes fixed on the perimeter gate.

A sudden blast behind them sent a wave of heat screaming through the air. A piece of burning metal whistled past Mike's ear, slamming into the ground with a hiss of steam.

"We're not going to make it!" Gideon yelled.

Mike grabbed Sarah's arm, yanking her forward. "We MAKE it!"

They burst through the shattered gates just as the earth shuddered violently beneath their feet.

A rumbling roar, deeper than anything human, rolled up from the compound. Mike turned just in time to see the ground split open, a final explosion ripping through the central core.

The blast surged upward, a monstrous pillar of flame punching into the night sky, lighting up the horizon like a second sun.

Mike flung himself over Sarah, shielding her with his body as the shockwave slammed into them.

Gideon hit the dirt beside them, arms wrapped around the drive, gritting his teeth as the heat scorched over his back.

The world became a storm of light, noise, and fury.

Minutes — or maybe hours — later, Mike lifted his head.

His ears rang. His mouth tasted like blood and smoke.

Beside him, Sarah groaned softly, blinking through soot-streaked lashes.

Gideon coughed, rolling onto his back, the drive still clutched in his hands.

"It's done," he rasped. "It's finally done."

But Mike wasn't so sure.

He pulled Sarah to her feet, his muscles screaming in protest, and turned to look at the smouldering wreckage.

The Watchers. Amy. The Prime.

All of it… gone.

Or so it seemed.

Because just beyond the haze, in the shadows, something moved.

A figure stepped into view — calm, composed, untouched by the fire.

A man they had never seen before.

He smiled.

"Well," the stranger said softly, "now the real game begins."

Mike's fists clenched.

Sarah's breath caught in her throat.

Gideon's eyes widened.

The fire was just the beginning.

And the next storm was already on its way.

Epilogue

The world smelled like cinders.

Mike stood at the edge of the ruined compound, the scorched earth still warm under his boots. Beside him, Sarah wrapped her arms around herself, staring into the smouldering crater.

They had done it.

They had destroyed the Watchers.

…Or so they thought.

A faint crackle echoed through the comm device in Mike's ear — faint, scratchy, but unmistakable.

Gideon's voice, low and grim:

"You're going to want to hear this."

Inside the wrecked remains of their temporary safehouse, Gideon sat in front of a battered laptop.

On the screen: a series of cascading data streams, files unlocking one by one.

He tapped a key, magnifying a set of encrypted files.

The title sent a chill through him: ARCHIVE SECTOR 9: SLEEPERS.

Names began to scroll.

Faces.

Locations.

Mike. Sarah. Mary. Jane. Even Gideon himself.

But below those familiar profiles were hundreds of others — people they didn't know.

People the Watchers had planted in cities, governments, companies, families.

Sarah's voice broke through the silence.

"What is this?" she whispered.

Mike's jaw clenched. "This… this wasn't the end."

Gideon nodded slowly. "No. We didn't kill the Watchers. We only exposed one branch."

He leaned closer to the screen.

"And now the others are waking up."

Miles away, in an opulent, hidden chamber, a woman in a white suit stood before a large wall of monitors.

She watched the feed from the compound collapse, fingers steepled under her chin.

Beside her, several shadowed figures waited — each one carrying the insignia of the Watcher Elite.

The woman smiled faintly.

"Prepare the next phase," she said softly. "They think they've won. Now, we teach them what it means to play on a global scale."

Back at the edge of the crater, Mike took Sarah's hand, his gaze hard.

"We finish this," he said.

Sarah looked up at him, firelight dancing in her eyes. "We'll need help."

Mike's mouth twisted into a grim smile. "Then we call in everyone. Old allies. New ones. Anyone who's ever had a score to settle."

Gideon's voice crackled through the comm again.

"And you're going to want to hurry," he murmured. "Because the clock just started ticking."

Book 4: BLOODLINE

The Watchers are bigger.

The betrayals run deeper.

And this time…

no one is safe.

Printed in Great Britain
by Amazon